HAPPY BIRTHDAY, POCO LOCO!

by **J. R. Krause** and **Maria Chua**

two lions

To Mrs. Paula Brown and Mr. Eric Hoover,
Jedi Masters of art education.

Endless thanks always to our parents and daughters.

J. R. Krause and **Maria Chua** are a husband and wife team living in Southern California.
Maria attended the University of Madrid, Spain, and lived in Mexico. She is a bilingual psychiatric
social worker in Los Angeles. J. R. is an artist, designer, and animator working in television.
Currently he is a designer for *The Simpsons*. They are also the creators of *Poco Loco*.
To learn more visit: www.jrkrause.com

Text and illustrations copyright © 2016 by J. R. Krause and Maria Chua

Published by Two Lions, New York
www.apub.com

Amazon, the Amazon logo, and Two Lions are trademarks of Amazon.com, Inc., or its affiliates.

ISBN-13: 9781477826386 (hardcover)
ISBN-10: 1477826386 (hardcover)
ISBN-13: 9781503947030 (paperback)
ISBN-10: 1503947033 (paperback)

The illustrations are rendered in digital media.

Printed in China (R)
First edition
10 9 8 7 6 5 4 3 2 1

GLOSSARY OF SPANISH WORDS

AMIGOS (ah-MEE-gos): friends

AYÚDANOS (ah-YOO-da-nos): help us

AZÚCAR (a-SU-kar): sugar

BUEN PROVECHO (boo-en pro-VAY-cho): enjoy your meal

CANCIÓN (kan-see-ON): song

CERDO (SER-do): pig

COLORES (coh-LOH-rehs): colors

DELICIOSO (day-le-see-OH-so): delicious

DULCE (DOOL-say): sweet

FANTÁSTICO (fan-TAHS-te-ko): fantastic

FAVORITO (fah-vo-REE-to): favorite

FELIZ CUMPLEAÑOS (fay-leeth koom-play-AH-ny-os): Happy Birthday

FIESTA (fe-ESS-tah): party

GALLO (GA-yo): rooster

GATO (GAH-toe): cat

GRACIAS (GRA-see-ahs): thank you

HARINA (ah-REE-nah): flour

HUEVOS (oo-AY-vos): eggs

LECHE (LAY-chay): milk

LOCO (LO-ko): crazy

MÁXIMO (MAHC-se-mo): maximum

MÍNIMO (ME-knee-moh): minimum

MUCHO MÁS (MOO-cho mahs): a lot more

NO HAY PROBLEMA (no ay pro-BLAY-mah): no problem

PASTEL (pas-TEL): cake

PERFECTO (per-FEK-to): perfect

PIÑATA (pee-NAYH-tah): piñata

POCO (PO-ko): little

POR FAVOR (por fah-VOR): please

QUE RICO (kay REE-co): how delicious

RATÓN (rah-TONE): mouse

SENCILLO (sen-SEE-yo): simple

SOFISTICADO (so-fees-tee-CAH-do): sophisticated, fancy

SORPRESA (sor-PRAY-sah): surprise

VACA (VAH-kah): cow

VELA (VAY-lah): candle

POCO is a very unusual RATÓN.
He invents wacky things like a Motorcycle Mop.
And his vacuum cleaner is a robot!

Everyone thinks he is one crazy mouse.
That's why they call him Poco Loco.

"¡F-E-L-I-Z C-U-M-P-L-E-A-Ñ-O-S!"
beeps Robo-Vacuum.

Today is Poco Loco's birthday.
He is planning the best FIESTA ever!

Poco Loco's AMIGOS are here!

"¡FELIZ CUMPLEAÑOS!" crows Gallo.
"I hope your FIESTA isn't like last year," meows Gato.
"My tail is still extra twisted," oinks Cerdo.
"The PIÑATA Propeller blew everything away," moos Vaca.

"Don't worry, AMIGOS," squeaks Poco Loco.
"This year my FIESTA will be PERFECTO."

He turns on his newest invention,
the Cake-Baking Bunk Bed.

"¡PASTEL!" crows Gallo.
"¡QUE RICO!" meows Gato.
"¡FANTÁSTICO!" oinks Cerdo.
"¡BUEN PROVECHO!" moos Vaca.

HUEVOS

"¡D-E-L-I-C-I-O-S-O!" burps Robo-Vacuum.

"We need another PASTEL," oinks Cerdo.

"NO HAY PROBLEMA," squeaks Poco Loco. He adds LECHE, HARINA, AZÚCAR, and HUEVOS.

"¡M-U-Y D-E-L-I-C-I-O-S-O!" burps Robo-Vacuum.

"M-A-S P-A-S-T-E-L, P-O-R F-A-V-O-R."

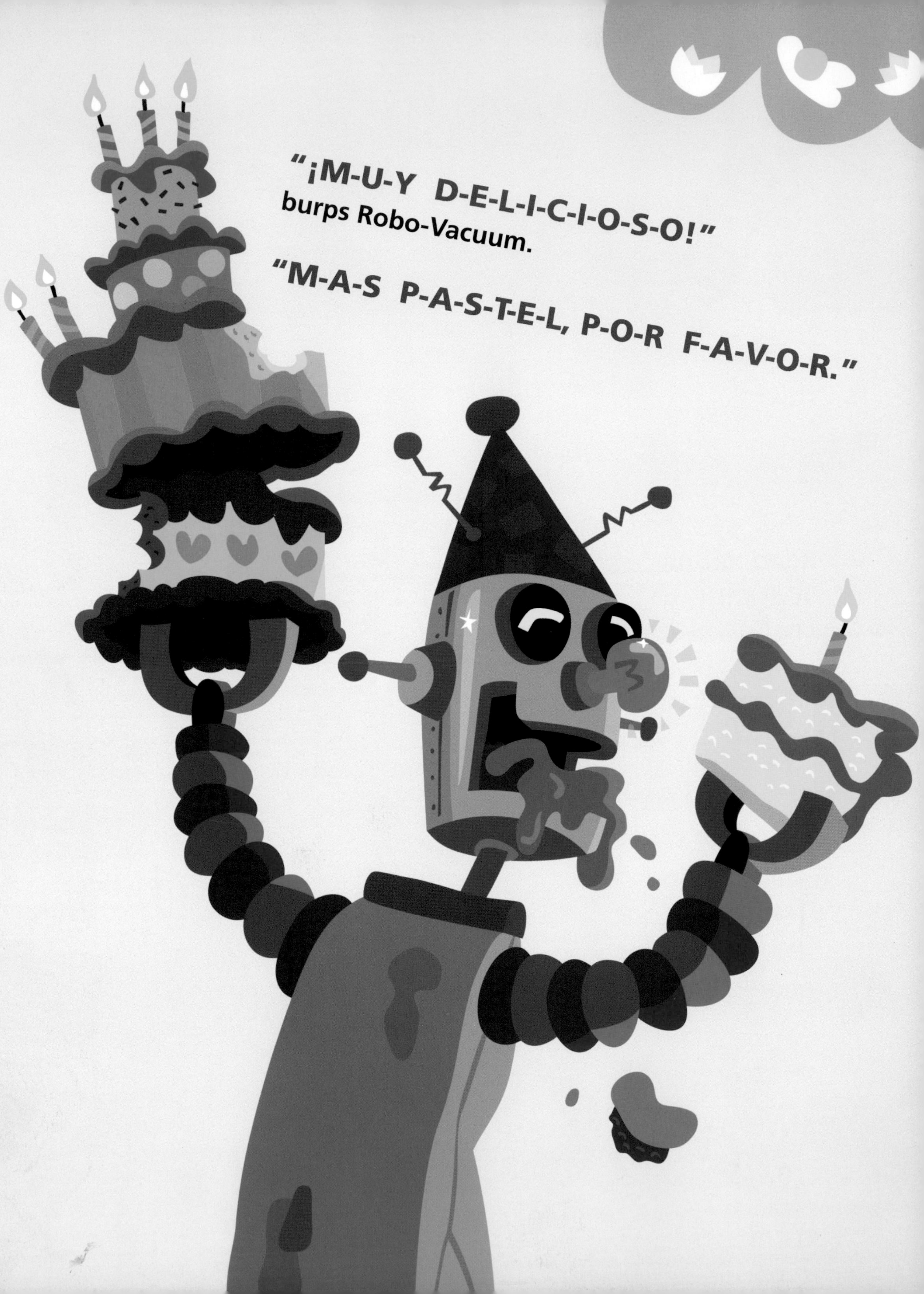

Robo-Vacuum
adds MUCHO MÁS
LECHE, HARINA,
AZÚCAR, and
HUEVOS.

It cranks the power to MÁXIMO.

"Where is GALLO?"

Poco Loco grabs Surfboard Slippers.
He lowers the Scuba Scarf until it almost disappears.

"Where is GATO?"

Poco Loco pulls out the
Pogo Pencil. He takes
a deep breath and
bounces into the PASTEL.

Poco Loco casts the Flashlight Fishing Rod and fishes in the frosting.

"Where is VACA?"

Poco Loco throws the Radio Rope.
He turns up the volume and squeaks
"¡VACA!" as loud as he can.

Robo-Vacuum also rises out of the cake and starts a giant sucking whirlpool.

"¡M-Á-S P-A-S-T-E-L!" "¡AYÚDANOS!"

"At least it hasn't asked for ice cream!" moos VACA.

"That's it!" Poco Loco remembers his other birthday invention.

"The Super Duper
Ice Cream Scooper!"

Poco and Robo-Vacuum clean up the mess.
"B-U-R-P!"

"GRACIAS, Poco Loco," shout Gallo, Gato, Cerdo, and Vaca.
"You saved the day!"

"But there's no more PASTEL," squeaks Poco Loco.
"My FIESTA is a disaster, just like last year."

"¡SORPRESA!" crows Gallo.
"We made UN PASTEL, but we hid it," meows Gato.
"And I lit LA VELA," oinks Cerdo.
"Now it's time for UNA CANCIÓN!" moos Vaca.

"¡FELIZ CUMPLEAÑOS, POCO LOCO!"

sing Gallo, Gato, Cerdo, Vaca, and Robo-Vacuum.

"¡MI FAVORITO!" squeaks Poco Loco.
"With lots of ice cream!"
"¡FELIZ CUMPLEAÑOS, Poco Loco!"